VOLLEYBALL *Dreams*

BY JAKE MADDOX

text by Jessica Gunderson

illustrations by Katie Wood

STONE ARCH BOOKS
a capstone imprint

Jake Maddox books are published by Stone Arch Books
A Capstone Imprint
1710 Roe Crest Drive
North Mankato, Minnesota 56003
www.capstonepub.com

Library of Congress Cataloging-in-Publication Data
Maddox, Jake.
Volleyball dreams / by Jake Maddox ; text by Jessica Gunderson ; illustrated by
Katie Wood.
p. cm. ~ (Jake Maddox sports story)
Summary: Ramona is very serious about beach volleyball, and she is frustrated
with her summer league team--but when she learns that a plastics company is going
to build a factory in their park, she realizes that it will take the whole team to try
and save their court.
ISBN 978-1-4342-3292-2 (library binding)
ISBN 978-1-4342-3907-5 (pbk.)
1. Beach volleyball--Juvenile fiction. 2. Youth protest movements--Juvenile
fiction. 3. Urban parks--Protection--Juvenile fiction. [1. Beach volleyball--Fiction. 2.
Volleyball--Fiction. 3. Protest movements--Fiction. 4. Teamwork (Sports)--Fiction.] I.
Gunderson, Jessica. II. Wood, Katie, 1981- ill. III. Title. IV. Series.

PZ7.M25643Vol 2012
813.6--dc23

2011032226

Designer: Heather Kindseth
Production Specialist: Michelle Biedscheid

Printed in China by Nordica.
0114/CA21400079
012014   007961R

TABLE OF CONTENTS

Chapter One

BETTER LUCK NEXT TIME

"Focus, guys," I yelled, trying to keep my team on track.

The ball flew over the net and spiraled over to our side. I bounced back, my eyes on the ball. My hands were clasped together and my arms flexed.

I glanced ahead of me and saw Scott and Teesha in position. When the ball fell toward me, I bumped it with my forearms.

So far, so good, I thought.

Scott jumped and set the ball to Teesha. All she had to do was spike it over the net, and we'd still be in the game.

But as the ball came toward her, Teesha took a step back. She flinched as she looked up at the ball. Then she held out one hand and gave the ball a little slap. It fell against the net and rolled back onto our side.

The Tigers cheered. They needed only one more point to win. I sighed and shook my head.

Beach volleyball was my favorite sport, and winning the match meant everything to me. My secret dream was to play beach volleyball in the Olympics.

But if my team, the Lakers, couldn't even beat the Tigers, how would I ever make an Olympic team?

I looked around at my five teammates. In official games like the Olympics, beach volleyball teams have only two players. But since this was a coed summer league, we played with six on a team.

I moved into position next to Teesha. "Why didn't you spike it?" I hissed to her.

Teesha shrugged. "The ball was coming at me so fast," she said.

"That's the point," I said. My voice was getting louder. "This is volleyball! The ball should come fast."

My brother Jack gave me a pat on my shoulder as he jogged past. "Cool it, Ramona," he said. "It's not over yet."

I looked over at Coach Kayla, who was giving me a warning eye. She knew how frustrated I could get sometimes.

"Come on, Lakers!" I yelled. "Let's make Lakeview proud!"

No one yelled back. In fact, I thought I heard one of my teammates snicker.

The Tigers launched the ball over the net. Jack bumped it to Scott. But this time Scott didn't do what he was supposed to. He tossed the ball right into the waiting hands of the Tigers, who volleyed it back easily.

I could see that no one on our side was ready. I dived forward, but I was too late. The ball plopped onto the sand.

My teammates stared down at it as the Tigers cheered. Only Jack looked disappointed.

"Do you realize that we just lost?" I demanded. "That was the Tigers' fifteenth point!"

Scott shrugged. "Oh well," he said. "The Tigers are a good team. We'll have better luck next time."

"Luck?" I asked. "It's not about luck. It's about skill."

Teesha giggled. "I think it's all luck with me. I don't have any skill."

"You're not even trying," I said. I turned my face so no one could see my tears.

We shook the Tigers' hands. "Good game," they said. But I knew they were just saying that.

"Come on, Ramona. Let's go home," Jack said.

But I was too angry. "Why are you even on this team?" I yelled at Teesha, Scott, Zac, and Avery. "You don't even care about winning!"

Avery turned to me. "My parents made me join," she said.

"Mine did, too," said Scott.

Great. So no one even wanted to play. And in a few days, we'd be playing our biggest rival, the Hilltop Hornets. How on earth would we ever win when no one even cared?

Chapter Two

BAD NEWS

Coach Kayla called us together for a huddle. She looked just as disappointed as I was. I thought she'd yell, but she didn't. Instead, she said, "Sit down on the grass, everyone. I have some bad news."

What could be worse than losing five games in a row? I thought.

"Okay, listen up, everybody," Coach said. "A new plastic factory is coming to Lakeview."

Jack and I frowned at each other. What did a factory have to do with beach volleyball?

"The factory will create new jobs," Coach went on. "But there is one bad thing. The factory will be built here. In the park."

"What?" asked Teesha.

"No way!" said Zac.

"What will happen to our court?" I asked, jumping to my feet.

"Everything in the park will be gone," Coach said. She looked at me. "Even the volleyball court."

"No!" I yelled. "It can't be gone. Where will we play?" Hot tears simmered in my eyes. No one understood what volleyball meant to me.

We had moved to Lakeview last year, and I'd been sad to leave my old friends. But then I joined the beach volleyball league. It was the one thing I was good at, and I made new friends. When I played volleyball, I forgot all about my sadness. What would I do without it?

"Well, construction starts a week from Monday," Coach told us.

"But the season won't be over!" I exclaimed. "What will we do?"

Avery and Teesha looked at each other, shrugging. "No more volleyball, I guess," Avery said.

"Maybe I'll join a kickball league instead," said Zac.

"Is there anything we can do?" Jack asked Coach Kayla.

She shook her head. "I don't think so. There was already a meeting with the city commission."

Scott jumped up. For a moment I thought he was getting angry too, but then he said, "My dad's here. Gotta go."

And one by one our team wandered away, until just Jack and I were left with Coach Kayla.

"No one even cares about volleyball," I said, plopping down onto the grass and putting my head in my hands.

"I care," said Jack.

"So do I," said Coach.

I wiped my tears and looked at Jack and Coach Kayla. "So, what are we going to do?" I asked.

"I got it!" Jack said with excitement.

"Got what?" I asked.

"We should have a protest," Jack said. "I saw it on a show once and it totally worked."

"That's a great idea," Coach said.

"I'll try anything at this point," I said.

Chapter Three

THE PROTEST

Jack and I spent all night making signs that read "Save Our Park" and "Leaf the Trees Alone!"

The next morning, we called everyone on the team to tell them about the protest. However, no one else seemed to care.

"Mmmhmm," said Teesha sleepily. "I'm busy."

"I'll try!" said Avery cheerily.

"I can't," said Zac.

"We'll see," said Scott.

But the next day, Jack and I were the only ones at the protest. We stood at the corner of the park and waved our signs at passing cars. A few cars honked and waved. But most sped on by.

After a while, Jack threw down his signs. "This isn't working," he said. "We should just go home. How are the two of us going to convince anybody?"

"You're right," I said with a sigh. "I guess my volleyball dreams are over."

"Maybe they aren't over," Jack said. "They're just on hold for a while."

"Same thing," I said as I grabbed our signs and started to walk home.

That night, I couldn't sleep. Outside my window, stars glimmered like grains of sand. And the full moon looked like a bright round volleyball.

I sat up, turned on my lamp, and got out my computer. "Dear Lakeview City Commission," I began to type.

I wrote for an hour, telling the commission all about my beach volleyball dreams. I told them how beach volleyball had helped me get through tough times after we'd moved to Lakeview.

I told them that my greatest sports hero was Kerri Walsh, Olympic gold medalist in beach volleyball. I even told them how I dreamed of playing in the Olympics someday.

I ended the letter by saying that beach volleyball was the only sport that my brother and I played together, and that destroying the park was like destroying our family.

If Jack ever read the letter, he would tell me how dramatic I am. But I knew what I'd written was true. I printed the letter out and set it on my desk.

In the morning, I read the letter again. *What good will this do?* I wondered. It's not like they'll listen to a kid. I crumpled up the letter and threw it in the garbage.

Chapter Four

THE NEW GIRL

We had one more practice to go before our game with our biggest rivals, the Hilltop Hornets.

"I've been looking forward to this practice," I told Jack as we were walking to practice. "We need to get the team back on track. We have a lot of work to do."

Jack couldn't help laughing. "You're so dramatic. It's supposed to be fun, remember?"

As we rounded the corner to the park, what I saw made me stop and gasp. A giant yellow monster was standing at the far end of the park. Well, it wasn't a monster exactly. It was a bulldozer.

"No!" I cried. I ran up to Coach Kayla. But she wasn't listening to me. She was on her phone.

She waved me away and kept talking. When she finally clicked her phone off, I started in.

"The bulldozer! What should we do? I thought they weren't starting until next week! What about the —"

But Scott interrupted me. "Hey, Ramona, look around," he said. "What do you see?"

I looked around, confused. There stood Zac, Teesha, and Scott.

"Avery isn't here!" I said.

"Avery quit," said Teesha.

"But we can't play with five people!" I said. "It's against the rules."

"Avery did quit," Coach said, "but I have a solution. And she's running this way!"

A girl with a long blond ponytail was running toward us.

"Am I late?" she asked, breathless.

"Who are you?" I asked.

"Don't be rude," Jack whispered.

The girl smiled. "I'm your new teammate!" she said.

"This is Bella," Coach Kayla explained. "She'll be playing with us for the rest of the season."

"The rest of the week, you mean, until they kick us out of the park to build that stupid factory," I muttered.

Teesha stepped forward to shake Bella's hand. "Hello, new teammate!" she said. "I'm Teesha."

"And I'm Scott!" Scott said, stepping forward, too.

I peered at Bella closely. "Wait a second," I said. She looked familiar. Very familiar. Then I knew where I'd seen her. "Aren't you a Hornet?" I asked, frowning.

Bella laughed. "I used to be," she said. "But we moved to Lakeview, so here I am! I guess now I'm a Laker!"

"Okay, everyone. Enough talking. Let's get this practice started!" Coach said. "We have a lot to teach Bella."

"I'm ready to learn!" Bella said. She shrugged off her hoodie and threw her bag to the ground.

Then I saw her T-shirt. It read "Save Lakeview Park!" On the back was an outline of the park, complete with its trees and our volleyball court.

"Hey, cool shirt!" said Zac.

"Oh, I almost forgot!" Bella said. She opened her bag and pulled out a stack of T-shirts. "Let's all wear these!" she said. "Maybe it'll help convince the plastic factory to build somewhere else."

Everyone grabbed a T-shirt, except me. "Don't you want one?" Bella asked me. I snatched one out of her hand.

"I guess," I mumbled. Why hadn't I thought of making T-shirts?

"And I was thinking," Bella said, "we could have a protest. We could make signs and march around the park."

"That's a great idea!" said Zac.

"And maybe we could make flyers and go door to door," Teesha suggested.

"I was going to —" I started, but no one heard me.

I glanced toward Coach Kayla. But she was on her phone again. I turned back to the team. Bella was still chatting away.

"Okay, team!" I yelled at the top of my lungs. "Let's play!"

Bella stopped talking and stared at me.

"Don't mind her," Teesha whispered to Bella. "She yells a lot. And I mean, a lot."

Chapter Five

ACE

During practice Bella played with Jack and Zac against Teesha, Scott, and me. When she served the ball, it sailed toward my corner, heading out of bounds. I was so sure it would go out of bounds that I didn't even jump for it.

But it landed with a plop on the corner. In bounds.

"Nice ace!" Jack congratulated Bella.

It was a good ace. But I didn't tell Bella that.

Since they won the rally, they served the ball again. Zac served underhand, but his ball went nowhere near our side. It launched crookedly upward then fell to the side.

"Come on, Zac!" I yelled. "We need to keep our serves in."

Bella walked over to Zac. "I see your problem," she said. "You're hitting the ball too late. Don't wait for it to drop to your hand. Instead, swing your arm up to hit the ball halfway. Then you'll get some height. And better aim, too."

"Try it again, Zac," Coach said, nodding.

"There wouldn't be any do-overs during a real match," I muttered.

Zac served and the ball came straight toward me. I bumped it to Teesha, who spiked the ball hard. It almost went over the net, but fell to our side.

"Come on, Teesha!" I groaned. "That was an easy spike."

Then Bella's voice sailed over the net. "Great try, Teesha!" she said. "Just a little higher next time!"

The next time Bella's team served, I was ready. I launched the ball over the net and, even though Jack and Bella scrambled for it, it plummeted to the sand. Score one for us!

"Excellent!" said Bella.

"Excellent?" I said. "We just scored a point, and you didn't. You shouldn't be cheering for us."

"We're teammates," Bella said. "We should always cheer each other on."

I turned away, tossing the ball to Scott to serve. As we played, Bella's smile got wider, and my frown got deeper. My team only scored two more points to Bella's six more points.

Finally Coach stepped up. "That's enough for today," she said. "I think we're ready for the big game tomorrow, huh?" She winked at Bella.

"Will you be at our protest this afternoon?" Bella asked me.

"I guess," I mumbled.

"I thought you wanted to save the park," she said.

I shrugged.

"What's wrong with you?" Jack asked as we walked home.

"What do you mean?" I asked.

"First, you complain that no one cares about volleyball," Jack said. "But Bella cares. And you don't like her."

"I never said that," I muttered.

"And Bella wants to save the park, but now you don't," Jack went on.

"I never said that, either!" I said. "I just don't like how Bella has taken over everything."

Jack was silent. Then he said, "You know, Ramona, you can't play volleyball alone."

Chapter Six

FUN IN THE SAND

That afternoon, I taped together one of my beat-up signs from the day before. Then I walked to the protest alone. Jack was already there, along with Bella and the rest of our teammates. But they weren't the only ones there. The whole park was filled with people and kids of all ages. Everyone was holding a sign.

"Wow," I said. Why hadn't all these people come to my protest?

I held up my battered sign and stood by myself at the end of the row of people.

This time, nearly every car that drove by stopped. Some got out and joined us. But the entire day, I didn't see Coach.

After the crowd dispersed, I walked toward my teammates. "I guess your protest was a success," I said to Bella.

"Hi, Ramona!" she said. "I didn't know you were here."

"Of course she was here!" said Jack. "This volleyball court is the most important thing in the world to my sister."

I turned to Scott, Teesha, and Zac. "Ready for the big match tomorrow?" I asked. "Get lots of rest. And fluids. Don't eat too much before the match —"

"Okay, okay," said Scott.

I knew I was being bossy, but I just couldn't help myself. I went on, "And Zac, if you can't get a good volley, set it up for someone else to hit. You always try for volleys you can't make."

Zac turned red.

"And Teesha," I went on, even though Jack was tugging on my arm. "Don't be scared of the ball —"

Bella interrupted me. "But the most important thing," she said, "is to have fun!"

"No, it's not," I said. "The most important thing is to win!"

"We can't win if we're not enjoying ourselves," Bella said.

I had no response. Maybe she was right, but I'd never admit it.

"We're going out for ice cream," said Scott. "Wanna come?"

I shook my head. I knew they didn't want me there anyway.

"You're not being a team player," Jack whispered at me. But I just glared at him.

After they left, I walked toward the beach volleyball court. Two little kids were throwing a Nerf volleyball high in the air, giggling. They were having a lot of fun.

"Can I play?" I asked. They nodded.

I tossed the ball over the net. I didn't care about form or stance. I didn't even care about hitting the ball out of bounds. I just wanted to have fun in the sand.

Soon, I was giggling just like the younger kids.

As I walked home, I had a lot to think about.

Maybe Bella is right, I thought. It was important to have fun. I liked to win, but not if it meant losing all my friends.

Chapter Seven

THE BIG MATCH

It was the day of the big match against our rivals, the Hilltop Hornets. The weather was perfect. I was nervous but excited. Jack felt the same way.

When Jack and I got to the park, I was amazed at all the people who'd gathered to watch us.

"Wow!" I said to Jack. "I've never seen this many spectators before!"

The Hornets were huddled by their coach. When they walked toward the court, I saw their shirts. "Save Lakeview Park!" the shirts read. The shirts were just like ours, but a different color.

"Okay, team," said Coach Kayla. "Let's have a good attitude and have some fun. We can win this!"

I knew she was talking to me. I vowed to have a better outlook. We got into our formation, and the referee blew the whistle to start the game.

We were playing three sets. The first team to make fifteen points would win the set. The first team to win two sets would win the match.

"Let's go, Lakers!" I yelled. "This is our game!"

Bella was the first to serve. The ball flew toward the back corner, but the Hornets were ready. One girl in the back passed the ball, and her teammate slammed it over. Jack lunged for it, but he was too late. The ball landed in the sand.

"One, Hornets!" called the referee.

"Come on, Lakers!" I yelled. "Let's do this!"

When I turned to rotate our formation, Bella was standing right behind me, offering her hands for a high-ten. I remembered my vow to have a better attitude. I slapped her hands and got into my place in the front row.

The Hornets served to us again. Scott set the ball for Teesha, and she knocked it over the net. A Hornet spiked it, but I was ready.

I jumped and blocked it. The ball swished to the Hornet side and fell through the Hornets' arms to the sand.

"One, Lakers!" cried the referee.

"Excellent block, Ramona!" said Bella.

"Thanks," I said.

Jack served the ball to the Hornets. They volleyed it back, but Bella set it for Zac, who spiked it over for a point.

We were ahead.

We kept our momentum going through the rest of the set, winning it by five points.

"They're good," I heard a Hornet mutter.

After the set, we took a break. As Coach talked to us, Bella swigged water from her metal bottle.

"I don't use plastic bottles anymore," she told me. "In protest of the factory."

I had to laugh.

"Do you want to help me hand out these flyers?" she asked, picking up a stack of papers.

I followed her through the crowd, handing out flyers to everyone, even the Hornets' fans.

"I'm worried about starting school in the fall," Bella confided. "What if I don't make friends?"

I couldn't believe my ears. Bella already had more friends than I did.

"I know how you feel," I told her. "I felt the same when we moved here last year. Volleyball helps, though."

Bella was silent for a minute. I took a deep breath and said, "And you already have one friend. Me."

Bella smiled at me. As we walked back toward our team, Bella whispered, "Can I tell you my secret? I really want to play beach volleyball in the Olympics someday."

"Really? Me too!" I said.

"Who's your favorite player?" she asked.

"Kerri Walsh, definitely," I said.

Bella smiled. "I like Misty May-Treanor," she said.

"They're Olympic teammates!" I said.

"Maybe you and I can be like Kerri and Misty someday," Bella said.

"That would be awesome!" I agreed.

Chapter Eight

THE SUIT GUY

I felt energized as we headed back toward our teammates. They were sitting near Coach Kayla, but she wasn't talking to them. She was on the phone again.

"We need a new coach," I whispered to Bella.

"Why?" she said. "Coach is doing all she can."

I turned to ask her what she meant, but the ref blew the whistle to signal the start of the second set.

As we tromped onto the court, I turned to the team with a smile. "Great effort last set!" I said. "Let's keep it up!"

"What's gotten into you?" asked Zac. "I've never seen you smile before."

"It's because we're winning," Scott said.

My smile dropped to my usual frown. "That's not —" I started.

"Stay positive!" interrupted Bella. "Let's grind the Hornets into the sand!"

But our momentum was gone. Even though we scored on the first rally, the Hornets blocked every attack we made for the next three rallies.

"Pay attention!" I growled to the team as we started the fifth rally.

"Work together!" said Bella.

The Hornets served the ball and Scott sent it back to them for an easy kill.

But the Hornets came back full force, knocking out three points. We managed to score four more, but before we knew it, they'd gotten fifteen.

We slogged toward Coach, exhausted.

But Coach didn't look exhausted. She didn't even look concerned. She had a bright smile on her face and was waving excitedly. "Ramona!" she called.

I noticed she was standing next to a man in a gray suit. Who would wear a suit to a beach volleyball match?

I walked toward them.

"So you're the one who's causing all the trouble," the man said to me.

I looked worriedly at Coach, then back to the man.

"Excuse me?" I said.

"I got your letter," he explained.

"What letter?" I asked.

Coach stepped forward. "Ramona, this is Matt Matterhorn," she said. "He's the owner of Matterhorn Plastics."

"Oh," I said. "But you must be mistaken. I didn't write a letter to you."

Mr. Matterhorn laughed. "No, you addressed it to the city commission. But it wound up in my mailbox."

But the letter was in my wastebasket at home. I hadn't mailed it. Unless . . .

I turned and saw Jack lingering nearby. He raised his eyebrows.

"Sorry, Ramona. I had to send it," he said. "It was too important to just throw it away."

"I agree! You have some big dreams," Mr. Matterhorn said. "The Olympics, even! But it's good to dream big. That's how I've achieved everything I have."

And by stealing people's parks, I thought.

"Your coach has been making some phone calls," Mr. Matterhorn went on.

"A lot of phone calls," Coach corrected.

"And she's convinced us to hold off construction until fall," Mr. Matterhorn explained.

Now it was starting to make sense why Coach was always on the phone.

"So we can finish the season!" I exclaimed. "But what about next year?"

Mr. Matterhorn shrugged. "My company is going to donate the money to build another park," he said. "People need a place to play volleyball, and you need to practice if you're going to make it to the Olympics."

"And for now, we have a volleyball match to win," Coach said, steering me toward our team.

"Good luck," said Mr. Matterhorn. "I'll be cheering for you."

Chapter Nine

ON A ROLL

"We didn't save the park," I told our team. "But we can finish the season, at least."

"Hurray!" said Scott.

I pulled Bella aside. "Thank you for everything you've done for our team. And our court," I said.

"It's my team now, too," Bella said. "And really, it was your letter that helped the most."

"I only wrote the letter," I said. "Jack is the one who actually mailed it."

I smiled at my brother, and he smiled back.

"Let's play!" I said to the Lakers. "And let's have fun!"

Teesha looked at me, surprised, and then gave me a high-five.

Maybe my team would end up liking me after all. As long as I kept my new attitude, anyway.

The set started. The Hornets served the ball and we sent it back to them.

A Hornet bounced it easily off his elbow, and his teammate launched it to us.

The ball plummeted quickly into our side. I ran forward. I would have to dive to hit the ball before it hit the sand.

I dove face-first, arms outstretched. I hit the ball as hard as I could. I had a mouthful of sand, but the ball was still active. But would anyone else get to it in time?

Jack was there. He set the ball and then Bella spiked it over, right into a Hornet void.

The first point of the set went to us.

"Awesome play, Ramona and Jack!" said Bella.

"You too!" we answered.

We scored on the next four rallies. It was 5-0.

And then it was my turn to serve. I slapped out an overhand serve, aiming for the far right corner like Bella had done during practice.

The ball dropped in bounds. My first ace, and another point for us.

We slapped hands as we got into position. The crowd was cheering. Mr. Matterhorn was cheering the loudest.

Our momentum was back. We were on a roll, and it wasn't going to stop any time soon!

About the *Author*

Jessica Gunderson grew up in North Dakota. She is currently a writer and teacher in Madison, Wisconsin, where she lives with her husband and cat.

About the *Illustrator*

Katie Wood fell in love with drawing when she was very small. Since graduating from Loughborough University School of Art and Design in 2004, she has been living her dream working as a freelance illustrator. From her studio in Leicester, England, she creates bright and lively illustrations for books and magazines all over the world.

GLOSSARY

ace (AYSS) — a serve that can't be passed by the receiving team

dispersed (diss-PURSST) — scattered

formation (for-MAY-shuhn) — the way the players on the team are arranged

kill (KIL) — a spike that results in a point

match (MACH) — a volleyball game, usually consisting of three or five sets of fifteen points each

momentum (moh-MEN-tuhm) — the force or speed that something is moving

protest (PROH-test) — a demonstration or statement against something

rally (RAL-ee) — a series of passes between teams until the ball is grounded and a point is awarded

rival (RYE-vuhl) — someone you are competing against

spectators (SPEK-tay-turz) — people who watch an event without participating in it

spike (SPIKE) — a forceful hit designed to drive the ball to the ground on the opponent's side of the net

DISCUSSION QUESTIONS

1. Ramona has troubles with bossiness. Why do you think she is so bossy to her teammates?

2. At first, Ramona resents the new girl, Bella. Why?

3. After Bella joins the Lakers, the team pulls together. Why do you think Bella's presence helps the team's attitude?

WRITING PROMPTS

1. Ramona and Bella dream of becoming Olympic beach volleyball players. Write about a dream you have for the future.

2. Bella is positive and friendly when she joins the team. But being the new kid isn't always easy. Write a scene from Bella's point of view.

3. In order to win, the Lakers have to work together as a team. Write about your experience on a team.

BEACH VOLLEYBAL FACTS

In 1895, William Morgan invented volleyball. Beach volleyball was originally played in the 1920s by surfers who were on the beach, waiting for good surfing waves. It was played with six players per team.

In 1930, Paul Johnson organized the first game of beach volleyball with doubles in Santa Monica, California. This changed beach volleyball forever.

Beach volleyball is similar to indoor volleyball, except that it is played on sand and the players are barefoot. Professional teams have two players rather than six.

American teammates Kerri Walsh and Misty May-Treanor won gold medals in the 2004 and 2008 Olympics.

Beach volleyball became an official Olympic sport in the 1996 Olympic Games in Atlanta, Georgia.

Beach volleyball is a popular summer league sport. Summer leagues are usually coed and have six players per team.

In the 1970s and 1980s, beach volleyball became more popular. It became a professional sport and spread worldwide.

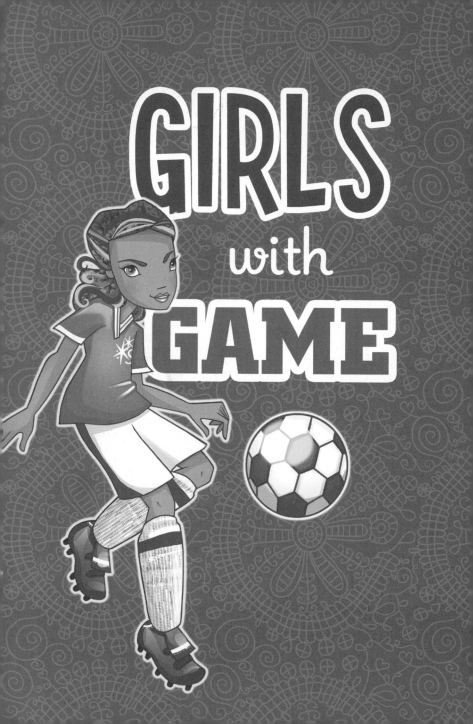

Read more
JAKE MADDOX
stories!